Disney

Peter Pan

Far away from here, there exists a place where the sun always shines, the sky is always blue and the people never grow up. This paradise is called Never Land, and it's home to Peter Pan and Tinker Bell.

In London, not far from Never Land, lived Wendy, John and Michael Darling. Each night, they would gather in their bedroom to hear Wendy's tales of Peter Pan, friendly Indians and the evil pirates of Never Land.

One day, as Wendy told John and Michael their favorite Peter Pan story, Nana, their Saint Bernard, began to bark in the yard. At that very moment, Peter Pan and Tinker Bell were climbing into their bedroom.

"I've come to find my shadow," said Peter Pan. "Nana took it from me last time I came to listen to your stories."

While Wendy mended Peter Pan's shadow, John and Michael watched their hero with admiration.

"I'm so happy that you came this evening, Peter," said Wendy. "It's my last night in the nursery. Starting tomorrow, I'll have my own room."

"But that means you won't tell any more stories!" cried Peter. "Come with me to Never Land!"

Wendy, John and Michael couldn't believe their ears. "We would love to!" they said.

Peter Pan took a pinch of Tinker Bell's pixie dust and sprinkled it over the children. He told them to think happy thoughts.

"You can fly!" said Peter.

They flew all night until they reached Never Land.

From up above, they could see a rainbow, waterfalls and a lagoon full of mermaids. It was the most beautiful place they had ever seen. There were beaches, forests and of course, an Indian village. They had finally reached Never Land.

"Come this way," said Peter, as Wendy, Michael and John landed in the middle of the forest. He led them to his secret hideout where he lived with his friends, the Lost Boys.

John and Michael played with the boys while Wendy and Peter went to visit Mermaid Lagoon.

As they crouched behind a rock, Peter and Wendy saw Tiger Lily, the Indian Chief's daughter. Captain Hook and Mr. Smee had captured her in a boat.

Peter and Wendy eavesdropped on the pirates.

"Tell me where to find Peter Pan!" demanded Hook, but Tiger Lily stayed silent.

"I have to save her," Peter whispered to Wendy. Captain Hook was bringing Tiger Lily to Skull Rock.

Peter and Wendy flew to Tiger Lily's rescue. A fierce battle broke out between Peter and Captain Hook. Suddenly, Mr. Smee cried, "Do you hear something?" It was the tick tock of the crocodile's clock, and he was headed right for them. "Help!" cried Hook. He lost his balance and fell into the water.

Peter swam to the prisoner and released her.

Captain Hook was furious. "That pesky Peter Pan! I'll get him once and for all!" he barked.

Hook had captured Tinker Bell and coaxed her into revealing Peter Pan's hideout. Then, the Captain trapped the little fairy inside a lantern.

In a hollow tree, the Lost Boys had gathered around Wendy. They listened intently to her marvelous stories.

Not far away, the pirates prepared to attack. When the Lost Boys and Wendy's brothers exited the tree, they were all captured.

When Wendy came out,
she saw that the pirates had
caught the boys. "Tie her up!"
yelled one of the pirates. They
captured poor Wendy, tied
thick ropes around her, and led
her through the forest.

"Peter Pan will save us!" said Wendy bravely.

Captain Hook laughed. "Peter Pan won't be able to save you," he scoffed. "You'll have to walk the plank!"

Nobody had realized that Tinker Bell had escaped the lantern. She flew to Peter Pan and told him all about Captain Hook's evil pla

Peter flew as quickly as he could to save his friends.

"This time, you've gone too far," Peter told Hook. "I'll teach you a lesson you'll never forget!"

Another battle ensued. Peter Pan threw Hook and the other pirates overboard, and a crocodile chased the Captain through the water.

"Hooray for Captain Peter Pan!" the boys cheered.
They would never again have to worry about Captain Hook.

The Darling children thanked Peter for saving them. "Could you tell me, sir, where we're sailing to?" Wendy asked politely.

"To London, madam," Peter replied.

"Come on, Tinker Bell!" said Peter. The children watched excitedly as Tinker Bell sprinkled pixie dust over the entire ship.

All of a sudden, something extraordinary happened. The vessel, which had turned a magnificent golden color, became as light as a feather in the wind. The ship sailed gently through the sky.

The ship drifted over the forest. The Indians couldn't believe their eyes as they watched it pass overhead.

"Can you hear it?" Michael asked.

"Hear what?" his sister replied.

"Big Ben chiming!" he cried joyfully. "We're home!"

Before returning to Never Land, Peter Pan and Tinker Bell promised never to forget Wendy, John and Michael. The children would certainly miss their friends, but they were delighted to be back home.